A PORPOISE FOR CARA

AUTHOR LINDA PENNINGTON BLACK

A PORPOISE FOR CARA

First print October 2012

Second print revised April 2016

Linda Pennington Black Author

Carol Dabney Cover Art and Illustrations

Published in the United States of America

ACKNOWLEDGEMENTS

I dedicate this book to all my children, Monique, Courtney, Tony, Stacy, Gary, Nykita and all the others who have touched my life and I theirs, in a special way. Life is a journey with many twisted paths, and it is my hope that this book will be a reminder to you to always be thankful for the many blessings and little treasures it has to offer.

Many thanks to Carol Dabney for the magnificent artwork, and for her commitment and diligence to get them done.

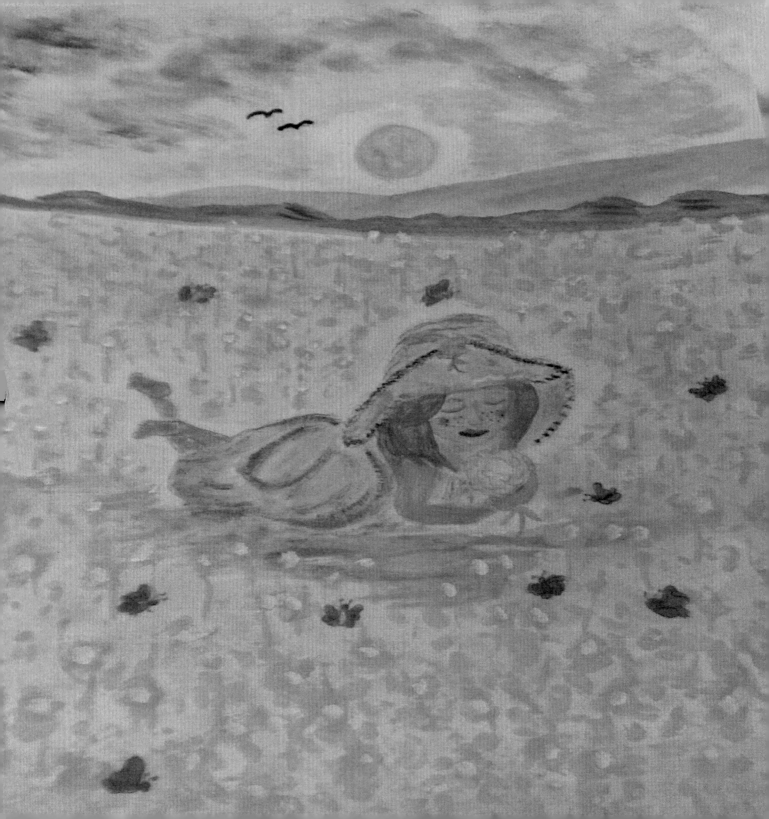

Cara Phillips was a beautiful red-headed girl with freckles. She lived with her mom, Elaine, on a large farm in South Carolina. Her father had passed away two years before, when she was only eight.

Cara was a loner. She would often lie in the meadows among the wildflowers and butterflies and daydream about going back to the ocean again, where they vacationed every year before her dad died.

After dark one evening, Elaine noticed Cara sitting with a blank stare gazing at the stars.
"What are you thinking about Cara? Penny for your thoughts?" Elaine smiled.

"I was thinking if there's a guardian angel for every star up there, we have more than enough to go around," said Cara.

"We never know who they are or when or where they'll show up, Elaine said as she patted Cara on the back. I have a surprise for you. We're going to the ocean tomorrow."

"Great!" Cara gave her a big hug.

Elaine and Cara arrived at their yacht just at the break of dawn. Soon they were pulling away from the dock. The ocean was calm and peaceful, but there was an aura of eerie quietness.

Cara played captain for about two hours while Elaine worked in the kitchen.

"Hey, are you about ready for some breakfast?" Elaine asked.

"Yes, being out in the open air makes me hungry," said Cara. They enjoyed quiche, melon and yogurt on deck.

"I've wanted to ask you something," Elaine said.

I hope she's not going to ask me again about not having friends. "What is it?"

"I'm concerned that you spend way too much time alone. I never see you talk to anyone, let alone hear you talk about having friends. What is the problem, honey?"

"I don't have any friends. The kids at school don't like me. They call me a stuck-up rich girl just because I'm quiet. I just don't fit in."

"Do you want me to talk to them?"

"No, Mom, it'll be all right.

Honey, I just don't like you being so alone and sad."

At that instant...a huge commotion and wild thrashing of water nearby could be heard, but they didn't quite know what was happening. When they moved closer, they could see it was a shark.

An adult porpoise was fighting a fierce battle for its life. They heard loud squeaking sounds and clicking nearby and turned to see an injured baby porpoise, a calf, trying to stay afloat. One of its fins looked badly damaged.

"We have to do something fast," Cara shouted. "Throw me that rope, Mom."

Cara threw the rope out to the porpoise, but he didn't catch on right away. He was flopping around aimlessly. They knew that time wasn't on their side. If they didn't hurry, the calf would be dinner for the shark too.

Cara hurled the rope again. The calf grabbed hold with its mouth.

"Help me pull it in, Mom. Hurry!"

They tugged hard, finally pulling the calf to safety just in the nick of time. The shark had spotted the calf and was rapidly swimming in its direction.

They needed to get help fast.

When they made it back to shore, they loaded the calf on the truck and headed out to find the nearest aquarium.

"I hope they have room for him there. He's going to need lots of care for a long time," said Cara.

"Let's just hope he survives," Elaine said.

The local aquarium was able to take him in, and Cara was happy. She visited him every day. Even after school started, she visited in the evening.

Cara named him "Floppy" after the way he flopped about with only one good fin.

"Hello Floppy, how are you today?" Cara asked. Floppy acknowledged as he flipped and wiggled.

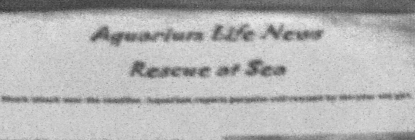

Aquarium Life News
Rescue at Sea

Shark attack near the coastline. Aquarium experts promise calf rescued by its new best pal.

Cora and her mother were able to rescue the young dolphin after witnessing a horrible shark attack on the adult porpoise off the shores early yesterday morning. The calf suffered injuries in the fight but is expected to recover. The newest member of the aquarium has been named Happy. Cora and her mother were able to get the young porpoise to grab a rope. Cora then jumped into the shark infested waters to pull the calf onto their boat. Nearby fishermen helped the family get the calf to the aquarium. The fishermen said that Cora's quick thinking saved the dolphin's life. Many are calling the little girl Cora "Happy's guardian angel." Cora says that Happy is her new best friend.

When the news spread about Cara's rescue of Floppy, she became very popular. Finally, she started to make friends.

A year passed, and Floppy grew stronger and stronger. He seemed to have forgotten his home was once the ocean. He seemed right at home at the aquarium. The handlers tried introducing him to the ocean, but he wanted no part of it.

Cara never missed a day visiting Floppy.
Over the next few years, Floppy grew larger and better than ever. The trainers were very impressed with some of his skills, despite his partial handicap.

It was graduation time, and Cara would be going off to college.

"Mom, what do you suppose will happen to Floppy after I'm gone?"

"I'm sure they'll take good care of him," she said. "You should be excited about your graduation and going off to college."

"I am, but I worry about him."

Before she left for college, Cara spent hours with Floppy. He seemed to sense that something was going on because he clung to Cara as never before. He eagerly showed off his new tricks.

Finally, she kissed him goodbye. "I'm going to miss you. You be a good boy now. I'll come see you as often as I can."

Six months passed before Cara came home. She couldn't wait to see Floppy.

Cara hurried into the house, gave her mom a nippy kiss, and rushed past her.

"Where are you off to so fast, young lady?" Elaine asked as Cara ran upstairs.

"I want to go see Floppy before it gets too late."

"Whoa! Slow down. It's not like he's going anywhere soon," Elaine said. "You just got here."

"I know, Mom, and I'm sorry for being so hasty, but I'm just so anxious to see him."

"I'll go with you," Elaine said.

Cara couldn't get there fast enough. "You'd better slow down, honey, if you don't want a ticket."

Cara rushed into the aquarium, and her mom followed. She looked around but didn't see Floppy. Her heart sank. She stormed into the office, "I don't see Floppy. Where is he? What did you do with him?"

"Hold on, Cara! He's in the training room. I'll let the trainer know you're here," said the secretary.

Floppy must have heard her voice because as soon as Cara entered the door, he was up chirping and showing off his newest tricks. As Cara squatted at the edge of the pool, Floppy dipped in. He surfaced with a big splash. Backing up on his tail, he showed off his new dance as she clapped.

"I was a little worried about Floppy when you first left, said the trainer. He didn't want to eat. I don't think he'll make it in the wild, Cara. He's practically lived his whole life at the aquarium. So with your permission, I'd like to continue to train him for the shows. He'll be a great act."

"That'll be great. He's made so much progress," Cara said.

Seeming to affirm what was happening, Floppy planted a kiss right on Cara's lips.

"He knows," said Cara grinning.

Each time Cara came home, Floppy had something new to show her.

Finally, he was ready for the water shows. At his first performance, Floppy assured Cara he knew she was there. He plunged deep into the pool and emerged with a mouth full of water, squirted her, and then danced away. Cara applauded.

"Oh my…he has…ah a new fin," she said beaming with pride.

"Yes, we thought we'd surprise you this time when you came," said the trainer. "He was fitted with it a couple of weeks ago and it's a perfect fit."

"He looks awesome."

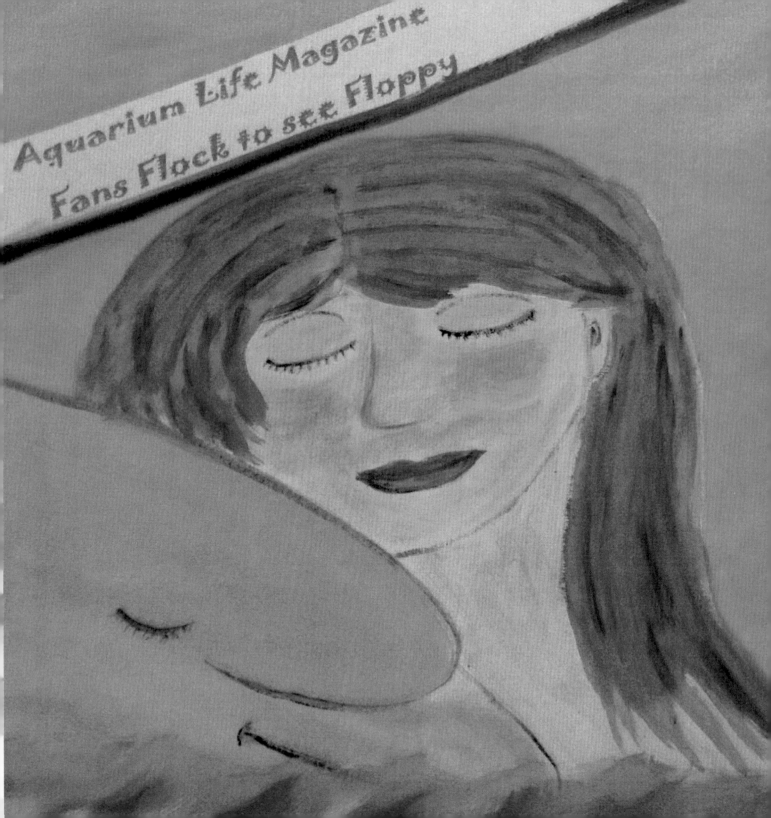

Aquarium Life Magazine

Fans Flock to see Floppy

As Floppy became famous, and eventually became the main attraction of the show, Cara made more and more friends.

Cara thanked her mom for taking her to the ocean that long ago morning because she couldn't imagine Floppy not being in her life or she in his. She thanked God, too, for putting her in the right place at the right moment and time.

As for guardian angels, Cara learned her mom was right:
"*You never know who they are or when or where they'll show up.*"

The End

ABOUT THE AUTHOR

Linda Pennington Black is a native Arkansan who grew up in the Arkadelphia community of Curtis, where she attended Curtis Industrial #64 through the sixth grade until the school's closing in 1962. From there she entered Peake High School in Arkadelphia and graduated from John Marshall Harlan High School in Chicago, Illinois. With her move to Lansing, Michigan she became gainfully employed with the General Motors Corporation for over thirty years.

During her stay in Michigan she chose Lansing Community College as her school for higher learning, where she attained an AA degree. She later joined the University of Phoenix to further studies in psychology and criminal justice.

At the tender age of 10, she wrote her first song. It was promptly sent off to Nashville to be set to music and even though it was not published, Linda never lost sight of her love for writing. She is a public speaker and an award winning author and poet. She has seven published books, a published poem in the anthology, Sistahs with Ink Voices, and a poem in the white house…written for President Obama's first inauguration. Find her books on Barnes and Noble, Amazon www.amazon.com/Linda-Black/e/B0056C44X6/ and bookstores everywhere.

ABOUT THE ILLUSTRATOR

Carol Dabney lives in Arkansas and Hawaii. She is an author, illustrator, speaker, composer, singer song-writer. She is the mother of five children. Carol has been a disc jockey and recorded in Nashville and with Tom Moffatt Productions in Honolulu. She has been a music resource teacher for twenty years and now presents her books and sings at schools and libraries across America.

If you want Carol to come to your program you can contact her by emailing at carol.dabney@yahoo.com or visit her website at www.caroldabney.com

Made in the USA
Columbia, SC
07 February 2019